Young Greta
La joven Greta

Young Animal Pride Series
Serie: Jóvenes Animales Distinguidos

Book 20
Libro 20

Cataloging-in-Publication Data

Sargent, Dave, 1941–
     Young greta = La joven greta /
by Dave and Pat Sargent ; illustrated by
Elaine Woodward. —Prairie Grove, AR :
Ozark Publishing, c2006.
     p. cm. (Young animal pride series ; 20)

     "I'm special"—Cover.
     SUMMARY: When a large bald eagle
tries to eat Greta, she realizes more than ever
just how important friends really are.
     ISBN 1-59381-272-8 (hc)
             1-59381-490-9 (pbk)
             1-59381-491-7 (pfb)

     1. Woodchuck—Juvenile fiction.
[1. Woodchuck—Fiction.] I. Sargent, Pat, 1936–
II. Woodward, Elaine, 1956– ill. III. Title. IV. Series.
     PZ10.3.S243Gr 2006
     [Fic]—dc21   2005906122

Young Greta
La joven Greta

Young Animal Pride Series
Serie: Jóvenes Animales Distinguidos

Book 20   Libro 20

by Dave and Pat Sargent

Illustrated by Elaine Woodward

Ozark Publishing, Inc.
P.O. Box 228
Prairie Grove, AR 72753

Dave and Pat Sargent, authors of the extremely popular Animal Pride Series, visit schools all over the United States, free of charge. If you would like to have Dave and Pat visit your school, please ask your librarian to call 1-800-321-5671.

Foreword

It is time for young Greta to leave home. Her days are full of surprises, like when a big bald eagle dives down for her.

Prefacio

Ya es hora de que Greta se vaya de su casa. Sus días están siempre llenos de sorpresas, como cuando un águila calva se lanzó en picada tras ella.

1

My name is Greta.

Mi nombre es Greta.

I am a groundhog.

Soy una marmota.

I live in the ground.

Vivo en la tierra.

My home is a burrow.

Mi hogar es una madriguera.

I am a big girl now.

Ya soy grande.

It is time to leave home.

Es hora de que me vaya de casa.

Here comes Robbie.

Aquí viene Robbie.

Robbie is my friend.

Robbie es mi amigo.

A bald eagle flew by.

Un águila calva pasó volando.

He circled overhead.

Voló en círculos sobre nosotros.

Baldy made a nose dive.

De pronto se lanzó en picada.

He shot straight down.

Iba derecho hacia abajo.

We ran fast.

Corrimos muy rápido.

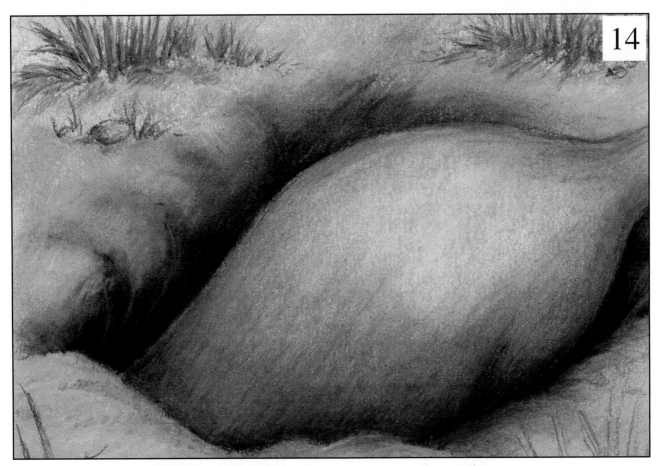

We fell into a hole.

Nos caímos en un hoyo.

Baldy Eagle missed us.

Nos escapamos del águila calva.

He was really mad!

¡Qué enojada estaba!

We landed in a burrow.

Aterrizamos en una madriguera.

No one lived there.

Nadie vivía ahí.

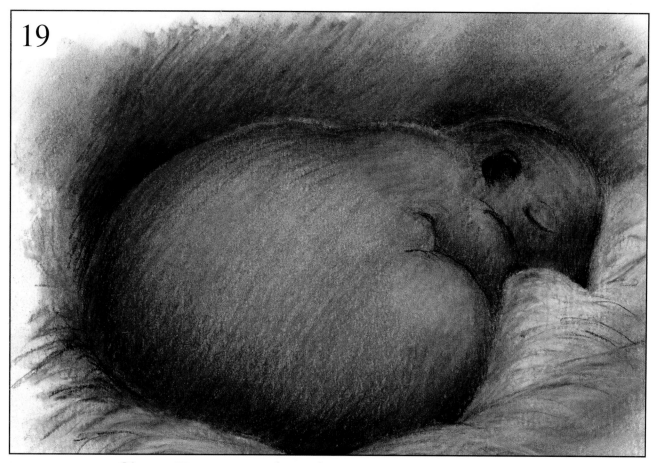

So I made it my home.

Así que la convertí en mi hogar.